DISNEY FAIRIES

Graphic Novels Available from
PAPERCUT**Z**

Graphic Novel #1

"Prilla's Talent"

Graphic Novel #2

"Tinker Bell and
the Wings of Rani"

Graphic Novel #3

"Tinker Bell and the Day of the Dragon"

Graphic Novel #4

"Tinker Bell to the Rescue"

Graphic Novel #5

"Tinker Bell and
the Pirate Adventure"

Graphic Novel #6

"A Present for Tinker Bell"

Graphic Novel #7

"Tinker Bell the Perfect Fairy"

Coming Soon:
Graphic Novel #8

"Tinker Bell and her Stories
for a Rainy Day"

#7 "Tinker Bell the Perfect Fairy"

Contents

PAPERCUTZ™

NEW YORK

"The Fairy Fashion Show"
Script: Paola Mulazzi
Revised Dialogue: Cortney Faye Powell
Pencils: Andrea Greppi
Inks: Marina Baggio
Color: Stefania Santi
Letters: Lea Hernandez
Page 5 Art:
Pencils: Caterina Giogetti
Inks: Roberta Zanotta
Color: Andrea Cagol

"No Need for Words"
Script: Paola Mulazzi
Revised Dialogue: Cortney Faye Powell
Pencils: Antonello Dalena & Manuela Razzi
Inks: Marina Baggio
Color: Stefania Santi
Letters: Lea Hernandez
Page 31 Art:
Pencils: Andrea Greppi
Inks: Roberta Zanotta
Color: Andrea Cagol

"Vidia Turns Nice!"
Script: Paola Mulazzi
Revised Dialogue: Cortney Faye Powell
Pencils: Caterina Giorgetti
Inks: Roberta Zanotta
Color: Stefania Santi
Letters: Lea Hernandez
Page 18 Art:
Pencils: Emilio Urbano and Manuela Razzi
Inks: Marina Baggio
Color: Andrea Cagol

"Tink, the Perfect Fairy!"
Script: Paola Mulazzi
Revised Dialogue: Cortney Faye Powell
Pencils: Antonello Dalena and Manuela Razzi
Inks: Marina Baggio
Color: Stefania Santi
Letters: Lea Hernandez
Page 44 Art:
Pencils: Caterina Giorgetti
Inks: Roberta Zanotta
Color: Andrea Cagol

Nelson Design Group – Production
Special Thanks – Jesse Post and Shiho Tilley
Michael Petranek – Associate Editor
Jim Salicrup – Editor-in-Chief

ISBN: 978-1-59707-281-6 paperback edition
ISBN: 978-1-59707-282-3 hardcover edition

Printed in Singapore. November 2011
by Tien Wah Press PTE LTD
4 Pandan Crescent
Singapore 128475

Distributed by Macmillan.

First Papercutz Printing

Tinker Bell and the Fairy Fashion Show

EVERYONE IN PIXIE HOLLOW IS TALKING ABOUT THE BIG NEWS! IT'S SO EXCITING! BUT THEY SAY THERE'S SOMETHING EXTRA-SPECIAL ABOUT THE NEXT FAIRY FASHION SHOW? WHAT'S THE STORY, TINK?

THAT'S EASY! THE SEWING-TALENT FAIRIES WON'T BE DOING ANYTHING!

WE EACH NEED TO MAKE OUR OWN GOWN! ONE JUST LIKE OUR TALENTS!

BUT IT'S DIFFICULT, TOO, PRILLA...

THE GOWN NEEDS TO REFLECT NOT ONLY YOUR TALENT, BUT YOUR PERSONALITY, TOO!

THAT SOUNDS LIKE FUN!

AND A SPECIAL JUDGE WILL PICK THE WINNER!

- 8 -

- 10 -

- 12 -

- 13 -

- 15 -

- 23 -

HM... I DON'T KNOW... DOES THAT SEEM LIKE THE RIGHT THING TO DO?

I WAS JUST THINKING THAT *MAYBE* IF SHE PRACTICED BEING NICE FOR A FEW DAYS, THAT MAYBE IT MIGHT RUB OFF ON HER...

AND WHEN WE CURE HER, THE VIDIA THAT WE HAD TO DEAL WITH ON A DAILY BASIS, WILL BE A LITTLE BIT NICER... PERMANENTLY.

FANTASTIC IDEA! THAT WAY SHE'D HAVE MORE FRIENDS AND SHE WOULDN'T BE SO ALONE!

BUT SHE WOULDN'T BE VIDIA...

I'M SO GLAD YOU GUYS AGREE! IT'S SETTLED THEN.

SINCE THEN, A NEW FAIRY HAS BEEN FLYING AROUND FAIRY HAVEN...

A KINDNESS-TALENT FAIRY, HELPING ALL WHO NEED IT...

...AND HER NAME IS *VIDIA!*

WHY IS VIDIA BEING SO NICE? WHAT'S SHE UP TO?

THUNK BANG SWISHHH

UH... THAT WAS VERY... VERY KIND OF YOU, VIDIA.

SINCE WHEN?

DON'T MENTION IT! IT'S MY SPECIALTY!

AND AGAIN...

THE MINER MICE PLAYING AND NOT WORKING...?

NOT IF THERE ISN'T ANTYHING FOR THEM TO DO.

VIDIA OFFERED TO DO THEIR WORK SO THEY COULD REST!

REST? THEY ONLY WORK ONE DAY A MONTH AND SHE HAS BEEN GOING AROUND...

...HELPING EVERYONE! I KNOW-- ISN'T IT GREAT? SHE'S PROBABLY MAKING UP FOR ALL THOSE TIMES SHE CAUSED HAVOC.

- 28 -

- 29 -

THE END

- 32 -

- 34 -

"I HADN'T TOLD ANYONE THE TRUTH... NOT EVEN TERENCE.

"HE DIDN'T KNOW THAT PETER PAN AND I HAD ONCE BEEN INSEPARBLE.

"HE DIDN'T KNOW THAT IT ALL ENDED...

"WHEN PETER BROUGHT THAT WENDY GIRL TO THE ISLAND!

"AND I HADN'T SEEN PETER SINCE."

I COULDN'T TELL TERENCE THAT I DIDN'T ASK PETER ABOUT MY HAMMER BECAUSE I WAS AFRAID OF SEEING HIM AGAIN.

BUT TERENCE CONVINCED ME TO GO SEE PETER. HE ACTED AS IF HE UNDERSTOOD EVERYTHING BETTER THAN I DID!

"HE MADE IT SEEM SO SIMPLE...

I COULD FLY WITH YOU TO SEE PETER PAN...

REALLY...? YOU MEAN IT?

WE'RE FRIENDS, RIGHT?

"I'D NEVER HAVE BEEN ABLE TO FACE PETER ON MY OWN...

"I WAS SO SCARED THAT HE'D IGNORE ME OR WOULDN'T EVEN REMEMBER ME!

"BUT WITH TERENCE BY MY SIDE, THAT GAVE ME COURAGE.

- 41 -

I DIDN'T WANT EVERYONE AT FAIRY HAVEN TO KNOW ABOUT PETER AND ME.

"BUT AGAIN, TERENCE UNDERSTOOD THAT WITHOUT ME TELLING HIM...

THE OTHERS DON'T NEED TO KNOW ABOUT OUR LITTLE TRIP, DO THEY?

YOU'RE A TRUE FRIEND, TERENCE! WHAT WOULD I DO WITHOUT YOU?

SO WHAT AM I DOING MOPING AROUND HERE?!

I'VE GOT TO MAKE THINGS RIGHT WITH TERENCE. I WAS THE ONE WHO WAS RUDE AND WRONG. SO, I'M THE ONE WHO SHOULD FIX IT!

I'LL MAKE HIM *FORGIVE* ME, NO MATTER WHAT IT TAKES! NOW ALL I HAVE TO DO IS FIND HIM...

Tink, the Perfect Fairy!

NO! THE *PERFECT FAIRY* WOULD HAVE TO BE AWESOME WITH ANIMALS--!

WHAT? YOU DID NOT JUST SAY THAT I AM BAD WITH ANIMALS?

NO! I'M SAYING YOU'RE NOT PERFECT!

ZIP YOUR WINGS! THAT WASN'T NICE!

YES, BECK, YOU SHOULD FLY BACKWARDS!

WHAT'S GOTTEN INTO ALL OF YOU?! STOP FIGHTING!

SPLASH

HEY, TINK... YOU OKAY? WE STOPPED FIGHTING... YOU CAN RETURN TO FAIRY HAVEN NOW.

HUH?

WHAT JUST HAPPENED?

I KNOW WHAT IT IS!

IT LOOKS LIKE THAT PEARL *EVAPORATED!*

WOULD YOU MIND TELLING US, THEN?

OKAY, BUT BRACE YOURSELVES...

WHAT JUST EVAPORATED WAS A *NEVERCHARM PEARL!*

I THOUGHT THEY WERE ONLY A TALL TALE!

A *NEVER* WHAT?

YOU'VE GOT TO BE KIDDING ME!

- 50 -

SQUEAK! SQUEAK! SQUEAK!

!!!

!!!

SQUIIRK!

SPLOOSH

I CAN'T BELIEVE MY EYES!

NOW, *THAT* IS HOW YOU GIVE CHIPMUNKS A BATH!

TINK, THAT WAS INCREDIBLE!

GOT TO FLY...

WHY WON'T YOU LISTEN TO ME LIKE THAT?

SQUEAK! SQUEAK! SQUEAK!*

!!!

*BECAUSE IT'S FUN TO SPEND TIME WITH YOU, BECK!

LATER ON...

IT DOESN'T SEEM LIKE TINK IS GOING BACK TO NORMAL ANYTIME SOON! I THINK IT IS TIME FOR US TO DO SOMETHING...

...SHE IS STEPPING ON EVERYONE'S WINGS!

I KNOW WHAT YOU MEAN. LOOK AT MY FIREFLIES, FOR CRYING OUT LOUD!

SHE CHANGED THEIR FLYING FORMATION-- AND IT LOOKS LIKE SHE MADE THE *PERFECT* CHOICE...

I SEE! BUT IT DOESN'T LOOK LIKE THE FIREFLIES ARE HAVING ANY FUN!

SHE TIDIED UP *MY* STUDIO! YOU KNOW I CAN'T BE INSPIRED WITHOUT MY CLUTTER!

I HEARD THAT SHE CHANGED ONE OF DULCIE'S RECIPES! CAN YOU BELIEVE IT?

AND I MUST ADMIT, SHE HASN'T EXACTLY BEEN FUN TO BE AROUND, EITHER!

LET'S FACE IT...

WATCH OUT FOR
PAPERCUTZ ™

Welcome to the seventh serendipitous DISNEY FAIRIES graphic novel from Papercutz. I'm Jim "the Sparrow Man" Salicrup, your award-winning[1] Papercutz Editor-in-Chief, and Pixie Dust Peddler!

We're all as proud as can be of this magical collection of DISNEY FAIRY tales—which features many moving and memorable moments. More than ever before we get to see Tinker Bell act all too humanly, even though she is a fairy. Her feelings are hurt when she doesn't win the cooking competition, yet she's conflicted when she has to judge the Fairy Fashion Show. She can't resist trying to change Vidia when the opportunity presents itself, yet when she tries to change herself and become the perfect fairy, she realizes that's impossible. (Yet, in her own way, to the millions of fans who love her just as she is—Tinker Bell really is "The Perfect Fairy.")

And if all that wasn't enough, we also had a super-special surprise guest—Peter Pan himself finally appears in the pages of a DISNEY FAIRIES graphic novel! If you thought his appearance was too brief, you'll be happy to know that he returns, along with Captain Hook, in DISNEY FAIRIES #8 "Tinker Bell and her Stories for a Rainy Day"! You don't want to miss it!

We also want to mention that if you enjoyed the beautiful artwork on "No Need for Words" and "Tink, the Perfect Fairy" that's probably because Antonello Dalena was one of the artists. If you like what you see, may I suggest another Papercutz series illustrated by Dalena that I'm sure you'll enjoy? It's called ERNEST & REBECCA, and it's the fun, and surprisingly touching tale, of a young girl and her best friend—who happens to be a germ! We think this new graphic novel series, available now at booksellers almost everywhere, is one of the best series being published in comics today! And a big part of that is the amazing artwork by Antonello Dalena—each and every page is filled with believable details, creating a world so real that you'll feel like you can step right into it! All I can say is that if you allow yourself to be exposed to ERNEST & REBECCA, the characters are so lovable, the humor so contagious—you won't be able to avoid being infected by them! (There's even a sneaky cameo appearance by a character we all love, as well as a zillion others, which makes looking at Dalena's artwork even more rewarding!)

(There's also another new series from Papercutz that Antonello Dalena and Manuela Razzi both illustrate. It's called SYBIL, and that's really all I can tell you about it—other that it's wonderful and magical and also available at better booksellers everywhere!)

Now that you know how much we love DISNEY FAIRIES #7— tell us what you think! You can e-mail me directly at salicrup@papercutz.com or you can send me an old-fashioned hand-written letter—just send it to Jim Salicrup, Papercutz, 40 Exchange Pl., Ste. 1308, New York, NY 10005. Or you can even visit us at www.papercutz.com.

So, until we meet again, don't forget to keep believing in "faith, trust, and pixie dust"!

Thanks,

Jim

[1] It's true! Jim won the 2011 CBG Fan Award for Favorite Editor! The Awards, sponsored by the Comics Buyer's Guide, and the voting is open to all comicbook fans. Jim thanks all the wonderful Papercutz writers, artists, colorists, letterers, designers, as well as Associate Editor Michael Petranek and Publisher Terry Nantier, for making him look good. And thanks everyone who voted for him as well—he greatly appreciates it.

Butterfly Wings

- 61 -

Don't miss DISNEY FAIRIES Graphic Novel #8 "Tinker Bell and her Stories for a Rainy Day"

Disney fairies

Discover the stories of Tinker Bell and her fairy friends!

Prilla and the Butterfly Lie

Queen Clarion's Secret

The Trouble with Tink

© Disney Enterprises, Inc.

COLLECT THEM ALL!
Available wherever
books are sold.
Also available on audio.